Create Your Own

GIRL BAND

JANET HOGGARTH

Scholastic Inc.

New York   Toronto   London   Auckland   Sydney
Mexico City   New Delhi   Hong Kong   Buenos Aires

To my sisters, Joanna and Katie,
who know how to party like
a real girl band!

ISBN 0-439-29651-X

12 11 10 9 8 7 6 5 4 3 2   1 2 3 4 5 6/0
                                          40

Printed in the U.S.A.
First Scholastic printing, July 2001

Contents

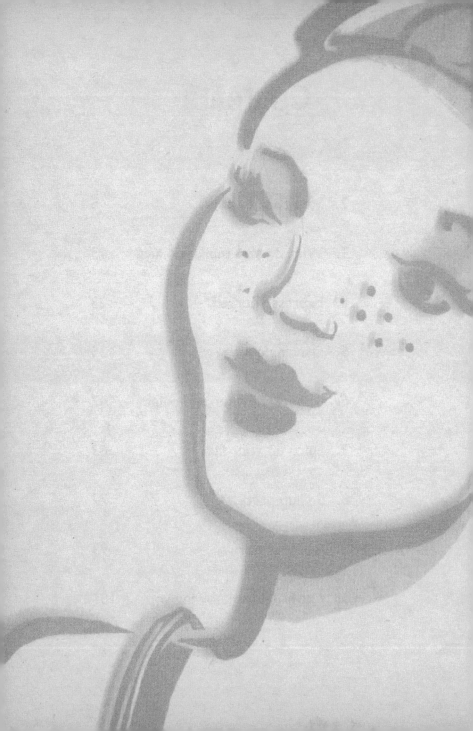

1.
Wannabe

Hey — we saw you! Singing into your hairbrush, thinking no one could see you. You were pretty good, actually; not bad for someone who dances like an electrocuted spider. You need some lessons there, girl! That's why we're here — to show you the way. We know you wanna sing, wanna dance, but why not do it with some friends? Why not think of a name, get some songs together, do some jiggy moves on the dance floor — form a GIRL BAND!

So how come *we* know so much? Well, you did ask. We are KandyFloz, the best and funkiest, maddest and baddest, grooviest and smoothest band to come along in . . . well, since girl bands began. You always need to be different, and we are cuz we have the fastest rapper in the world — MotorMouth LaydeeB — who makes us laugh with her awesome speed. But don't cross her, or you might end up a quivering wreck — she has a tongue as sharp as a viper's bite! It's time to come and say hi to us, your girl band guides — we'll be showing you how to get it together as the coolest chicks on the block.

Kym
Age: 14
Star sign: Aries
Pets: canary, lizard, two fish, and a hamster called Mr. Pig
Loves: popcorn, Destiny's Child, dancing, sunshine, holidays, and her mom
Loathes: rain ("it makes my hair frizzy!"), all rock music, meat, and peas
Most embarrassing moment: "Wetting my pants from laughing so much in math class!"
Motto: Go for it!

Skye
Age: 14
Star sign: Gemini
Pets: her little brother
Loves: pizza, running, singing, any dance music, art, makeup, and the movies
Loathes: fish, Backstreet Boys, and Furbies
Most embarrassing moment: "My leotard ripping in a school gymnastic display!"
Motto: Get there first before anyone else.

Fazza

Age: 13

Star sign: Capricorn

Pets: a dog called Dave
(for real – Dave the dog!)

Loves: Madonna, her dog, her family, chocolate, singing, and peanut butter

Loathes: burger bars, jazz music, cauliflower ("gross!"), sunburn, and boys who are jerks!

Most embarrassing moment: "Walking in dog doo and tracking it through the whole school!"

Motto: Just be happy!

MMLaydeeB

Age: 15

Star sign: Sagittarius

Pets: No way! They are for dweebs.

Loves: fashion, writing, Reese's Peanut Butter Cups, going out, Eminem, and her trendy sunglasses

Loathes: rude people, dark chocolate, eggs, Celine Dion, falling over ("I always do it!"), and oranges

Most embarrassing moment: "Realizing I had forgotten all the words to a song I was singing in the school play and having to get the script to remember it . . ."

Motto: Life's too short to be embarrassed!

Right — the book starts here! It has everything you need to know from hairstyles to stage shows, from funky diva clothes to manic makeup. If we can't make you look like a million dollars by the end of this book, I promise I will give away my sunglasses.

 And you know how much she loves those sunglasses! You girls had better be cooler than all the boy bands put together.

That won't be hard!

 Ooooh!! You meany.

2.
Step back in time

I'm the resident expert on our favorite Girl Power performers. Take a trip with me and check out the icons through the mists of time — Girl Power didn't all start with the Spice Girls, you know. There were girl music sensations as far back as the time before dinosaurs . . . well, the 1930s.

The Stone Age

Gasp, shock, horror! Yes, the 1930s and '40s. But they didn't sing pop, no sirree, it was good old Big Band music. The Andrews Sisters were the Destiny's Child of their day and were masssssssssive during World War II. They were still going in the 1960s, singing old classics like "Jingle Bells" and "Underneath the Arches."

Then came the 1960s! It was all change, all change! Girls were forming groups left, right, and center. And Motown was the coolest sound around. Thigh-length boots and miniskirts ruled the school . . .

The sixties, maaaan

The famous producer (well, ask your 'rents) Phil Spector gave us groups such as the Crystals ("Da Doo Ron Ron," "Then He Kissed Me" — you *must* know those! Your old man will for sure!), and the Ronettes, who warbled the megahit "Be My Baby." Another girlie act from the sixties was Martha and the Vandellas, whose hit "Dancing in the Street" was covered by aging rockers Mick Jagger (or rather Mick Jowler) and David Bowie for the historic concert Live Aid. Were your 'rents in the crowd? Gladys Knight and the Pips also dominated the charts throughout the sixties and seventies and well into the eighties.

The Shirelles had probably the most well-known hit, "Will You Still Love Me Tomorrow," but it's the Supremes who are the biggest-selling Girl Super Group EVER — even after all this time. Fronted by

Diana Ross, now a superstar in her own right, they stormed the charts with every release they made. The most famous was "Stop! In the Name of Love."

Now you know you wanna search out your 'rents old records to listen to those original girl bands, don'tcha? They have some banging tunes...

It happened first in the seventies . . .

He-he-he-he-he-he-he-heeeee! The seventies — glitter, flares, platforms, satin hot pants — no, really, all this happened before we were born, but look at how little has changed! You just aren't anyone at the moment if you don't have gold eye shadow. So slap it on and check out these superstars of the stompin' seventies.

The seventies was the disco decade but didn't have as many girl groups as the sixties or even the next decade — the eighties. But there were a few who really stood out from the crowd as glitter queens. The Pointer Sisters strutted their stuff through the seventies and the eighties with a string of disco hits including "Jump (For My Love)" and "I'm So Excited."

Joining them in sisterhood was Sister Sledge, famous for the disco classic "We Are Family."

The biggest cheese of the seventies wasn't a girl band, but a girl-boy band. They have to be mentioned because they're the influence behind beloved bands such as S Club 7, Steps, and Boys+Girls United, who are all big stars today. Of course, we're talking about ABBA! ABBA, from Sweden, won the Eurovision Song Contest in 1974 with the now famous "Waterloo." They were the supergroup of the decade with number one singles all over the world — "Dancing Queen," "I Have a Dream" (covered by Westlife), "Mamma Mia" — the list is endless. Without them, where would all those copycat groups be today?

Lace and crucifixes – the eighties . . .

This is where things start to get interesting. The eighties had the New Romantics — glitter, frilly shirts, lots of makeup — but that was just for the boys! Us ladies didn't want all that trash — we went for lace, fingerless gloves, and big hair that looked like it had been superglued in a hurricane. Way to go . . .

Well, the eighties saw girls scale new heights and pave the way for the explosion of female performers in the nineties. Yeah! The Go-Go's had hits mostly in the US. Singer Belinda Carlisle left the group to start a successful solo career with ditties "Heaven Is a Place on Earth" and "We Want the Same Thing." Another girl group to make waves was the Bangles. They had tons of hits, like "Walk Like an Egyptian" and "Eternal Flame."

The UK's biggest girl band before the Spice Girls was Bananarama. With hair like back-combed mohair sweaters and scruffy clothes, they were like our big sisters. Their hits included "Talking Italian" and "Shy Boy." This threesome still managed to slam-dunk the charts with hits even after a member left and was replaced by a friend of the band.

If Bananarama were the sweets of the British scene, then Salt 'n Peppa were the savory US girl rap duo. These girls had attitude and weren't afraid to show it! Originally telephone sales girls, they had huge hits with "Push It" and "Twist and Shout!"

We've just got to include someone else, even though she's not a girl group. She's had enough image changes, hairstyles, hit singles, and various scandals for at least ten girl groups put together: Madonna! The Queen of Pop was responsible for the lace fingerless glove and crucifix craze of the eighties. Hmmm — was that a good thing? Her popularity endures as she is still the number one female performer ever, churning out hit after hit.

Another chameleon girlie performer who was big in the eighties but is still banging out records today is Janet Jackson. She released her first album at the age of sixteen and was a real contender for Queen of Pop, but that title was already taken . . .

Snapping at the heels of Madonna were teen sensations Tiffany, who performed in shopping malls across the globe, and Debbie Gibson, who went on to make her name in theater. These teen songstresses set the standard for the nineties' and the new millennium's obsession with finding younger and younger stars for the teen music market, either as groups or as solo performers . . .

All that spice . . .

So, we are now in the time of our heroines. The nineties was the decade of Girl Power and the time when us laydees took over the charts before we'd even finished school. Awesome!

All was quiet on the girl front for a while. We had En Vogue and TLC (still going strong), but it was boy bands such as New Kids on the Block, Take That, and Backstreet Boys who ruled the charts. Yawn . . . But then one day I turned on the radio and out came this sound, like nothing I had ever heard before. *Zigazig haaaaaaa . . .* The Spice Girls! From then on we had Ginger telling us about Girl Power — sooooo cool. "Wannabe" stormed to number one across the world and the rest is history. Even when Geri left to be a successful solo artist, the Spices kept charging on with those hits. Nothing could stop the wave of girl bands that was about to swamp the international charts. This is OUR time!

After the Spices came All Saints with "Never Ever," then B*Witched with "C'est la Vie." After that, a wave of teenage girl groups and girl-boy groups descended upon us. Wow! Now let me see, there's Britney Spears, the biggest teen star of the moment; Christina Aguilera, Britney's rival; and S Club 7, brought to us by the ex-manager of the Spices. Also, Samantha Mumba, Steps (ABBA sound-alikes), Boys+Girls United, Girl Thing (apparently the next Big Thing in girl bands), Brandy and Monica and their counterpart in the UK, Cleopatra. There's Destiny's Child (the next big girl group), the Honeyz, obnoxious duo Daphne and Celeste (they are scary, sisters!), Mandy Moore and Jessica Simpson, and many, many more teen stars, all too numerous to mention . . .

PSST! Gossip Britney nearly joined girl band Innosense before she made it big.

Where will it end? Let's hope it doesn't. All these acts are dancing their way into the Millennium along with us, KandyFloz! Now you can see that girl bands are not a new phenomenon. But it isn't until now that we have made it BIG TIME and showed the world what Girl Power is all about. We rule!

3. Who do you think you are?

Well, you've seen the competition, past and present. Has it inspired you? It did me. I just know you chicas are gonna want to get it together as funky divas, sing those songs, and slam-dunk the funk on the stage to all your fans. But first, you gotta have a name, don'tcha?

Yeah! BUT before you even think about a name, do you and your posse have what it takes to be IN a girl band? Could you handle being away from home and always being on the road with no little corner of your own? Life's not always a bowl of cherries! Don't say I didn't warn you . . .

PSST! Gossip There's no escape from school, even when you top the charts! Mandy Moore does all her schoolwork over the Internet to keep up to date. ZZZzzz.

Are YOU girl band material?
Try this tough test:

1. How often do you need to see your closest buddies?

a. Every day — what else is school for?

b. As much as possible — at least every other day.

c. Doesn't matter, as long as you can call them.

2. Could you handle long periods away from home?

a. Maybe, but you might get homesick.

b. If it meant you'd be a superstar, then you guess so.

c. Not yet, you like your home comforts too much.

3. Would you get all starstruck if you met a celeb?

a. Yes. You'd love it but probably get really nervous.

b. No, not at all. They are human, aren't they?

c. Maybe at first, but then you'd have to snap out of it.

4. How much does your own space mean to you?

a. Everything. If you can't be on your own sometimes, you go crazy.

b. Depends upon how you feel — sometimes it's important, but not always.

c. Not much. You hate being on your own anyway.

5. Could you perform even when you're not in the mood?

a. You guess, but you probably wouldn't be much good.

b. Of course! You are always in the mood!

c. No way. Sometimes you just want to go and watch TV.

PSST! Gossip Some advice from UK girl band Cleopatra: "Don't be a 'genie in a bottle' like Christina Aguilera! Don't wait for someone else to change things, stand up for yourself! But don't be too harsh, or no one will respect you for it."

Did you pass go?

Results: 1) a. 0 b. 5 c. 10 2) a. 5 b. 10 c. 0 3) a. 0 b. 10 c. 5 4) a. 0 b. 5 c. 10 5) a. 5 b. 10 c. 0

If you scored 0–15

Hmm. You're not sure, are you? You prefer chilling at home with your friends and family to buzzing around the country singing and dancing. There's plenty of time for playing the fame game later on, so don't sweat.

If you scored 20–30

You've definitely got potential for life as a girl band member, but right now you are happy with your life as a normal kid. Just keep practicing those dance moves and high notes!

If you scored 35–40

You've got all the makings of a chart-topper! Try to keep your feet on the ground while you whirl around in a rush of gigs and photo shoots. But remember to have fun and take time to chill, sister!

PSST! Gossip The UK's answer to Britney, Billie Piper, has had old school friends selling stories about her to the papers. That's what you have to put up with if you're famous. Still want to make it big?

Do you think you've got what it takes to be in a girl band? Endless interviews, photo sessions, makeup calls, shows, no time to be yourself. Would you turn into an Ego-monster or be the Princess of Pop . . .

Pop or flop?

1. You are stuck in traffic on the way to a live TV show. It looks like you have no time for full makeup. Do you:
a. Have a major fight with the driver, blaming him — you look foul without makeup!

b. Plead with the makeup ladies when you get there to powder away your shiny nose?

c. Makeup isn't everything — your performance is what matters.

2. You are in an interview and get asked to comment about someone who has been bad-mouthing you. Do you:
a. Diss her too and say what a lowlife she is? If you can't beat 'em, join 'em!

b. Say she really hurt you and you think she is just jealous?

c. Don't say anything — you don't care what she says cuz you know it's not true.

3. You do a photo spread for a magazine and are allowed to approve the pictures. Do you:
a. Get them to airbrush your face — you don't want people to see all your pimples.

b. Choose one you like and say they are not allowed to use any of the others?

c. Let them choose — as long as you don't look too hideous, you're cool with that.

4. During a TV show performance, your pants split, but there's no time to do a retake. Do you:
a. Demand a retake even though you know it will ruin the time schedule of other acts?

b. Refuse to dance with the rest of the band in case you look stupid, but carry on singing?

c. Try not to laugh, and act like nothing's happened — you might make the headlines!

5. You have to study for an exam but were invited to a cool celeb party. Do you:
a. Go to the party, stupid! Who cares about exams, you're a pop star!

b. Study like mad for a few hours and then go out. You need a break.

c. Stay in and study? You might not be a pop star forever.

6. You are having dinner in a restaurant with your family and a fan wants you to pose for a picture and get your autograph. Do you:
a. Get really angry and shout at him to go away? How dare he interrupt your meal!

b. Reluctantly sign the autograph, but no to the picture — you are having a private night.

c. Pose for a pic and sign your napkin — you've always got time for fans.

7. It's your best friend's birthday and you are on tour with the girls. Did you:
a. Forget completely? You don't have time to remember things like that anymore.

b. Remember at the last minute and call her on the day to say her present's in the mail?

c. Arrange for her to come to the show and take her out for a meal after the concert?

PSST! Gossip Irish teen star Samantha Mumba has this to say about fame: "It's crazy being recognized everywhere you go. People's attitudes towards you change; all of a sudden people want to do things for you. I don't like that. It's a little mad."

Are you beauty or the beast?

Mostly A's

Oh, no! You are a pop brat! You're not too old to be locked in your bedroom with no supper, young lady. You won't last long with that bad attitude!

Mostly B's

You manage quite well with the pressures of fame and a normal life. Sometimes you can be a bit of a madame, but only slightly. That Princess of Pop crown is almost yours.

MOSTLY C's

You are a true Princess. Britney looks like a wild child compared to you. You have your feet firmly on the ground and just wanna have fun. After all, isn't that what it's all about?

PSST! Gossip A Britney fan decided to brighten up dull physics lessons by creating a web site at www.britneyspears.ac. As well as all the usual info, the site has

Britney's Guide to Semiconductor Physics, using her curves to illustrate mathematical equations!

Name in one

Sisters, you should be well on the way to realizing your potential as future stars, and this is when you really have to get it together on the name front. Here are some ideas to help you come up with something stylish for your act.

Drop of a hat

Well, this sounds very obvious, but sooo easy. Gather your girlies around you and get chilling with some drinks and snacks and pens and paper. Now write words on pieces of paper that you think are inspiring or funky or funny — whatever! Use film titles, song titles, TV programs. Try some of these:

Fresh * Funky * Chicas * Girlies * Glitter * Strawberry * Orange * Blue * Berries * Kandy * Street * Rain * Star * Red * Fluffy * Ice * Crew * Posse * Alert * Gold * Passion

Just look at some of the names of other bands:

> ❋ Girlz ❋ Pineapple ❋ Swirl ❋ Zoom ❋
> Silver ❋ Attack ❋ Machine ❋ Killer

Backstreet Boys, Westlife, True Steppers, Atomic Kitten, The Cardigans, Blink 182. How hard can it be to come up with a name?

 Are you kidding — we hung around for days before we thought up anything that didn't sound ridiculous!

Well, yeah — it can be a bit of a pain, but it has to be done. But you can make it fun. When you have written down as many words as you can think of, put them all in a hat.

Once the words are all in the hat, just take turns to pull one out and try it next to another word someone else pulls out. If it doesn't work right away, at least you can giggle about how stupid you would sound with a name like PuffCorn or FunkyBerries. The first name we tried was GetFresh, which I thought sounded like a cure for bad breath!

GIRL BAND

Did you know . . . ?

Hey — not all bands get their name right first time. Even solo performers have changed their original names to stage names to sound cooler. See if you can work out the original names of the ones we know.

a. B*Witched   Johnny and the Moondogs

b. George Michael   Pizzaman

c. The Beatles   The Tranzlator Crew

d. Destiny's Child   D-Zire

e. Fat Boy Slim   Girls' Town

f. Fugees   Yorgos Kyriacos Panayiotou

Answers

a. D-Zire b. Yorgos Kyriacos Panayiotou c. Johnny and the Moondogs d. Girls' Town e. Pizzaman f. The Tranzlator Crew

PSST! Gossip H from Steps is really called Ian Watkins and used to get called Swotkins at school!

So that's it — you know what you're in for and you have your name — next you need some songs.

Rock on to the next chapter . . .

22

4.
Express yourself

 Before you even think about choosing or writing any songs, you have to find out if you can actually sing!

Move your lips

Nearly all bands have a lead vocalist, so one of you needs to have a reasonably strong voice. Beyoncé is the strongest singer for Destiny's Child, and Jo and Rachel are the main singers with S Club 7. You will notice that most bands tend to mime when on TV — but only because their dance routines are so hectic that they can't do both without passing out. But look at Britney and Madonna — they sing and dance at the same time, we are sure you can too! Try these top tips for improving your voice:

★ Stand up straight with your feet not too close or too far apart, your shoulders relaxed, and your arms hanging lightly by your sides. Take a couple of deep breaths and clear your mind. This does take a bit of concentration!

★ To see what notes your voice can achieve, hum a low note and as you are humming start to speak a word in the same key as you are humming, like you are singing it. Hmmmmmmm-tomatoes . . . Or any word you like! Now try a bit higher doing the same thing, humming and speaking. Keep on going higher and higher until you can't go any higher or your voice sounds like a dying cat's! You should practice these all the time and you will notice that the more you repeat them, the higher you will eventually be able to reach.

★ Another way to make your voice stronger is to start with the humming, but this time open up the sound (very technical!) by singing the vowels from the alphabet: a e i o u. So try: Hmmmm-aaaaaa, hmmmm-eeeeee and so on, repeating from the lowest key to the highest you can reach.

Singing for real

In the second half of this chapter, there are ideas on how to choose songs and what to look for, but for now we need to concentrate on singing technique!

✦ You've got a song you want to sing as a group. If you are covering an old hit from another artist, really listen to the tune and see where the artist emphasizes words while singing and try to copy that.

✦ You will have to organize which one of you will sing which parts of the song, and if one of you does have a stronger voice, she should really sing lead vocals.

✦ All of you should learn the words by heart, but to really get the melody in your head, sing it without the words (on a "la" or an "ooh" basis!). That way you learn how your voices fit together and you will also be aware of where the breaks are so you can take breathers — vital for strong singing!

✦ Practice, practice, practice — the most important piece of advice ever! Now you are ready to sing the words and the melody. Go with it, fill your head with the song, and let go, so that what comes out of your mouth feels like the most natural thing in the world. And hopefully it will sound like it too . . .

Next up is songwriting. You may groan and think it's too much for you, but that's why we're here — to show you it ain't as hard as you think. Yeah! Just sit back and relax.

Writing shouldn't stress you. It's fun! And you don't have to write your own stuff at first — give these ideas a whirl . . .

Music for wrinklies . . .

We know you laugh at your olds' choice of tunes, but they are worth sniffing out. Lots of girl and boy bands cover tunes from yesteryear. Westlife covered an old ABBA slowie, "I Have a Dream," and Samantha Mumba sampled "Ashes to Ashes" by David Bowie for her big hit, "Body to Body." What you are looking for is something that has a catchy chorus and is basically very simple and easy to learn. Look for stuff from the seventies and eighties — old disco songs are always a winner. ABBA is a brilliant band to copy and so are the Jackson Five — their tunes are so catchy and easy to make up dance moves to — in fact, S Club 7 sound a bit like the Jackson Five.

If you want to cover an old tune, find it in your parents' record collection and then buy it as a karaoke CD. That way you have the music and lyrics separate, so you can either add your own words or use the original ones from the song sheet.

PSST! Gossip Did you know that Tina from S Club 7 used to sing with Shola Ama before she nearly joined another band altogether. Phew — close call!

WWW.lyrics . . .

If you want to use other bands' lyrics but maybe add your own to them, that's also cool. If you want to cover a song that you heard in your olds' CD collection, but can't find the words — fear not! Look up lyric sites on the Net. This one is good: **www.lyrics.ch/index.htm.** Just about everything is on there, including chart music, so you can cover fave girl band tunes as well.

PSST! Gossip Posh Spice on singing at home: "I can really go for it in the shower cuz no one can hear me and if I sound like a cat then that's fine."

It's easy when you know how . . .

You might be feeling brave and try to write your own songs. But what do you write about? How about some pop star advice . . . Daphne and Celeste, pop duo: *"Your songs should be about any kinda stuff — like your friends, your worst teacher, or anything that makes you laugh."*

Hello — isn't that a bit obvious? Well, yes, but it

is the best way to think about writing your very own songs. The Number One Rule about writing anything — stories or songs — is to write about what you know. The Spice Girls' first number one, "Wannabe," was about friendship. Daphne and Celeste's song "Ugly" was about bullying. Billie's first song, "Because We Want To," was just about having a good time. So what do you know about?

Have a band powwow to discuss your "artistic direction"!!!! Pens, paper, soda, and cookies are all vital ingredients to any serious songwriting venture. And then get to work.

Unless you are all accomplished musicians and have instruments, the best thing is to use the music of another song and just write your own lyrics. But of course, if you can play music, then go for it, girls! Or just sing without music, making sure the melody is a really strong tune.

It's in black and white

So, back to getting those words down on paper. Write down words like this and see where they take you.

> friends laughing parties
>
> game crying
>
> dancing playing together bullying
>
> disco sharing
>
> chicas standing falling over!
>
> up for you giving
>
> loyalty birthdays smiling

Just writing down random words can spark off all sorts of ideas and start you on the path to that first song.

Once you've got some ideas, write them down. Pick a subject and choose a tune you want to go with, say Britney's "Baby One More Time." Get a long piece of paper and count out the number of lines in the song. Then each of you takes a turn to write a line about the subject matter until you have a finished song. A really goofball way of writing is to fold over the paper after you have written your line so the next member of the band can't see. When you have finished the correct number of lines, unfold the paper and see what you've got. It might be total junk, but it might just be a stroke of genius! You never know.

The chorus is really important when you're writing a song. You can make it rhyme, but it doesn't really matter. If you look at most song lyrics, they don't always rhyme. BUT — if you want to create rhymes, say, if you're going to do a rap like LaydeeB and you are stuck on a word, check out this web site: **www.writeexpress.com/online.html** — it's awesome! All you do is type in your word and press "search" and it comes up with a zillion words that rhyme with it. Cool!

And if you're going to be really professional, you need to write a bridge. It's a couple of lines just before the chorus, to connect the last verse with the chorus. You could write the bridge like a short rap.

Don't forget when you "sing" a rap, you don't actually sing it, you are speaking, but not like you're reciting a shopping list! You gotta give it some oomph and attitude and rhythm. Be bold, be loud, and above all, do it with confidence. You can see an example of bridges and choruses and how they work in our song, "We Say."

We know girls who run and hide
But we can't do that
We got pride.
There's no point worryin'
What folks say
When all you wanna do is go out and play.

(Bridge)
Hey!
We're KandyFloz
Say!
Look who's boss.

(Chorus)
You wanna run with us
You gotta learn to be cool
Cuz we are the girls who rule the school.
No one here can take our place
So come and join our funky space.

Don't be scared cuz we don't bite
We just like
To give the boys a fright.
If they can't take it
That's just tough
We love to scare them with girlie stuff.

(Repeat bridge and chorus)

So, girls, let's hang out
We got lots
To shout about.
We're closer than sisters
And that's the thing
That makes us wanna get up and sing.

(Repeat bridge and chorus twice to fade)

You don't have to start with the first verse — you can start with the bridge and chorus if you like. Or you could have the chorus repeated only once — it's totally up to you. But if you *are* following a well-known tune, you should keep to that song's structure.

We haven't talked about writing or reading music because that really is way too complicated for this book! Not all pop stars who write their own tunes can read or write music, so we felt that for now, you could live in ignorance! What is important here is that you can at least sing and dance!

PSST! Gossip Oh, no! Make sure you know all the words before you go onstage. Poor Nicole from All Saints forgot the words to "Never Ever" at a HUGE concert in Hyde Park, London, in front of 100,000 people. We bet her face was cooking!

Now all you need to do is tape yourselves singing your song, so you can hear how harmonious you sound. Borrow a tape recorder and, if you can, a microphone and play your background music and give it all you've got. So — do you sound better than Britney and Christina?

If you want to have that true professional touch, make a tape cover for your recorded songs. Buy a throwaway camera and take pictures of all of you in stupid poses, get a parent to organize the developing, and then cut out your faces, the goofy poses, and paste them on to a tape cover with a wacky design in the background and your name on there somewhere. Now you've got your first album!

5.
Dancing queen

Hey! Get your boogie shoes on — we're gonna show those boy bands what we're made of! Don't worry, you don't have to do anything complicated — a routine only has to be a few moves to complement the song you are singing. No need for acrobatics and swinging from the ceiling, we just wanna have fun and mess around to music.

I lurve dancing. But trying to get a routine together when Skye keeps staring off into space is infuriating.

Just watch your mouth, missy! I can groove.

Yeah, yeah. Well, here are a few tips from your resident shoe shuffler and back-flip expert. Yes — *me*.

Kym's guide to not falling over . . .

✳ Don't try anything complicated at first. Make it as simple as possible and maybe when you get used to dancing together you can pull a few fast moves!

✳ If you are doing a slow number, dancing will look way over the top. All you need to do is keep moving on the spot in time with each other. Even just swaying from side to side is cool. Standing like a statue will look too weird. Just chill and go with the flow.

✳ Obvious — but make sure you are wearing shoes you can dance in. We don't want any accidents . . .

✳ Check out all the videos you can to get ideas for funky moves. Watch as many Britney, Spice Girls, S Club 7, Steps, and even those boy bands like Backstreet and 'N Sync. They always have amazing dance routines; but remember — they have been doing it for years and are superfit. You might end up in a sweaty heap if you try to copy and sing at the same time. Know your limits!

✳ Finally, when you are onstage and one of you forgets the exact move, don't just stand there — everyone will be watching you! Make something up and try to get back in the routine as soon as you can.

PSST! Gossip Billie Piper has a secret phobia: "Before I go onstage, I get really scared my shoes are gonna fall off . . . I have to tie them really tight, to make myself feel better."

Come on and move your body

So you've studied your videos and have an idea of what you want to do. Before you even start anything, have the singing all worked out so that when you do the routine, you can work around who is singing what part of the song. That way, someone who is being swung around upside down and thrown into the air (get real!) won't be singing at the same time. Might get messy!

Here's my number one easy way to start a routine. All of you stand with your backs to the audience, with the person who starts off singing at one end of the line, then the rest of you following in order of who sings next. Turn around to face the audience one by one as you sing your part until you are all facing the same way.

If you watch all the Billie and Britney videos, you will notice one move that is a real favorite of theirs — the one-legged side shuffle. If you want it to look mega cool, you need to do it all in time.

Move 1

◆ Get your posse lined up with two in front and the other two or three behind them, but to the side so they can be seen too.

◆ To make this easy, start off facing the front with both legs together and feet on the floor. Take a step to the right with your right leg and then bring the left leg over to join it like you are stepping sideways. Do that for four steps and then change and come back four steps to the left to where you started. That is all the move is, but funked up a little!

◆ Follow these instructions for the actual move in all the pop videos. Start by running on the spot at a steady pace — not so fast that you collapse from exhaustion before you've even started. When you have a rhythm going, try dropping a little more weight on your left leg, so that it looks like you have a limp!

◆ Now, as you drop your weight onto your left leg, move your right leg to the right like you did when you were walking sideways. The minute your right foot touches the floor, bring your left foot over to join it so you have taken a sideways step to the right. When your left foot is on the ground, taking most of your body weight, move the right leg over to the right and repeat.

◆ All the time you are running sideways with your

left leg taking most of your body weight and your right knee kicking out to make those shuffle-hops across the stage to the right. Your hands can go on your thighs, or you can move like you are running with a very fluid motion.

◆ Summary: Start, feet together — then step to the right, bring left leg to join right foot, then step again to the right and bring left foot to join right one. Do this for about four beats across the stage and then change and go back the other way to the left, this time putting all the weight on the right leg and bending the left knee.

If you want a move to go into right after this one, try this jump. When you have finished side hopping, the two dancers in the front jump down onto one knee and lower their heads so that their foreheads are touching their knees. Next, the two girls in the back run towards them and leapfrog over them with their legs as wide as they can go. The minute the girls have jumped, the other two stand up and join them, ready for what's next.

Another quick way of moving in between moves: Everyone turn out of their moves and get into a line. Turn back to back with another member of the band to form two or three couples. Now sidestep once right then left and repeat a couple of times together. A bit cheesy, but it can fill a gap in the routine.

Move 2

◆ Everyone stand back to back — again in pairs — and link arms with the person behind you.

◆ With arms linked, some bend over forward, lifting the other one off the ground onto her back with legs in the air. The person bent over is taking the whole body weight of the other, so make sure you are equally matched for size! While up in the air on the back of your partner, keep one leg pointed and one leg bent.

◆ You can swap by lowering back down to the floor

quickly but still with linked arms, and then repeating it with the other person who was supporting you. It will be quite hard to sing and do this, so perhaps do it when there is a break in the vocals.

 This is one of the first moves we did as a group, and if done exactly in time it looks better than Backstreet!

Move 3

◆ Everyone stand in a line with your left side facing the audience, leaving about a foot and a half of space between you. Bend over forward slightly so that you can touch your knees.

◆ Put your arms out in front of you with your hands outstretched like you are going to clap. Then jump back about three feet, still bent forward slightly while bringing your arms back with you, closing your hands so it looks like you are grabbing something and pulling it. You can jump back as many times as you like — but don't fall off the stage!

◆ To link this with another move or to jump the other way, when you have finished the final jump back, jump around to face the front and stand up straight, then jump around to face the other way and get in the position to jump back the other way. Sounds complicated, but it soooooo isn't.

 You can do lots of variations on this move. Instead of jumping back with your legs together, you could all stick one leg out in front of you and then alternate to the other leg when you do the next jump back. You can also do the move forward instead of backward and do different things with your arms. There are no rules. Just make it look funky!

 Hey! No one's mentioned the karate Sporty Spice kick! Jump up from your right leg then land on your left while kicking out your right leg out to the front. Girl Power!

Move 4

◆ Two of you stand in front and two behind and to the sides. Start running in place slowly to get the rhythm.

◆ In your head, chant "right, left, right, left," for when you land on the right or left leg, and this will make it easier to do the move. It's not a hard move to try, but this does help — honest!

◆ So — get down to the move! Start on your right leg, left leg, right leg and, instead of landing on left leg again, kick it to the side like a karate kick. Hi-yaaaaaa! To go back the other way and kick the other side is soooooooo simple. After you have kicked out the left leg, land on it and count that as left, then right, then left, then kick out your right leg and back again until you get extremely bored and have to think of another move.

◆ Summary: right, left, right — kick left leg; left, right, left, kick right leg. Move your arms however you like — just keep balanced.

This kick can look funked-up when done as a routine, but kicking your leg to the side instead of to the front.

Ladies — don't use all your moves in one routine. It will look too busy and no one will know where to look. And also, you will get so out of breath you won't be able to sing.

Yeah, these are by no means all the moves in the world, but I think you guessed that! The best thing is to make up your own by adapting what's here and what you see in pop videos — they're not hard to copy. That way, you should have enough for a zillion routines. Practice, practice practice!

6. Lipstick, powder, and paint

It's makeover time. Get ready for an image overhaul and a whole new you emerging from what was once a shy girl. First of all, we are gonna take a peek at makeup and what a laugh it is.

What's in the bag . . . ?

These basic items are what any girl band member absolutely cannot live without if she is to have that star-quality look!

* ❋ Sheer lip gloss
* ❋ Glitter!
* ❋ Eye jewels
* ❋ Cream blusher
* ❋ Tinted moisturizer
* ❋ Pressed powder

* Nail jewels and nail polish — all crazy colors are welcome!
* Gold bronzer for that Caribbean holiday look
* Eye gloss (or Vaseline if you are on a budget)
* Eye pencils in different colors
* Three-in-one color pot or stick for lips, eyes, and cheeks

So — what look you girls gonna go for? Individual looks like the Spices, or a similar group look like All Saints? Rude girls like Daphne and Celeste, or sleek and funky like Britney and Samantha Mumba?

You got the look

For makeup, what look you can carry off best all depends on your skin tone and eye color. Here are some basic color tips to get you started, cuz you don't want to look like a horror movie now, do you?

Eye . . .

Blue eyes Try browns; shades of blue, but not the same as your eye color, and a shimmery white or lilac.

LIPSTICK, POWDER, AND PAINT

Green or hazel eyes Peach, mauve, shimmery gold, purple, and silver all look great on you.

Brown eyes Shimmery golds and bronzes look great, as do stronger colors like greens and plums.

Lips and cheeks . . .

Fair skin Pinky-brown lipsticks and gloss and a warm pink blusher.

Asian skin Deep reddish brown lips or deep purple-pink and beige blusher.

Medium and olive skin Deep pink or plum lips and peach-brown blusher.

Black skin Deep plum or brown lips and plum blusher.

 Now that you know what color should suit your skin, it's time to mix it up funky style with those makeup brushes and see what look suits you girls best. But first, you need to know the best way to slap on the new you . . .

Number one tip!

Always put on a tinted moisturizer first to give yourself a healthy look — you might be a bit pasty during those winter months. Make sure you rub it in carefully or you could look streaky! If you have a shiny nose, you might want to dab it with the pressed powder that should be the same color as your skin.

Bat those eyes

The secret to gorgeous eyes is not to cake eye shadow on. Even if you are using bright colors and glitter — less is more!

✴ For glamour eyes, sweep a shimmery shade over your lids, with a lighter shade, like silvery white, over your brow bone to highlight. Or you could try glitter.

✴ Eye jewels are the same as body jewels but smaller. Stick them on the outer corner of each eye with eyelash glue (not *real* glue!) if they are not self-adhesive. An alternative if you can't find eye jewels is to stick sequins on instead.

✴ For that dewy Britney look, blend a bit of your fave eye shadow with eye gloss or Vaseline and apply to your brow bone.

✴ If you are feeling confident, draw a line on your top lid with an eyeliner color a bit darker than your eye shadow. Liquid liner gives a very hard line and is only recommended for those with a steady hand. Nothing worse than that wobbly eye look. Oops . . . Better to use a soft pencil or an applicator brush to apply it instead. Gorgeous, baybeeeee!

✴ Finally — only use this if you promise not to poke it in your eye! Mascara will make your lashes appear thicker and stand out from the rest of your eye. Brush it on in upward strokes. Never do the bottom lashes unless you go for the panda look. Don't go mad and put a million layers on, either, or it will look like spiders are crawling out of your eyes.

Pinch those cheeks

★ For that sun-kissed look, lightly brush bronzer on the very tops of your cheeks by your eyes, on your forehead, chin, and along the top of your nose. Now you will look like you have come back from a very tropical video shoot!

★ Before you apply your blusher, pinch your cheeks to see exactly where you blush naturally.

★ Use your finger to apply the cream blush where your skin has reddened slightly and blend the color gently, sweeping upwards towards the bronzer. Be careful not to drag the skin.

★ Glitter can glide along those cheekbones too.

Pout those lips

✦ Preparation is everything! Smear your lips with Vaseline and then rub an old toothbrush over them to get rid of flaky skin. Wipe it off.

✦ Apply a sheer gloss for a glamorous look, making sure it doesn't bleed over the edge of your lips. Sheer means that the color is not as strong as lipstick and looks more natural.

✦ If you are going to use lipstick — use a lip brush. It will be easier to apply an even look without smudging. If you are going to gloss your lips, put extra gloss in the center of both lips.

✦ If you can't afford both lipstick and gloss, just cheat by mixing up your fave lipstick with a blob of Vaseline.

✦ You can even add glitter to your lips and go glitter mad, but don't have it on your cheeks and your eyes at the same time! Not very sophisticated, daaarling!

PSST! Gossip Beyoncé from Destiny's Child knows all about too much lipstick: "I had bright red lipstick on, and I didn't realize it had gotten on the microphone while I was singing. I was rubbing the microphone everywhere and got lipstick all over my face!"

All that glitters is gold !

Don't forget — you can add gold even when you have other colors on. It goes with almost anything. Highlight your cheekbones, brow bones, and put it

LIPSTICK, POWDER, AND PAINT

on your lips too. If you want to look like a million dollars, when you have put on your outfit, dab gold body cream/highlighter on your shoulders and shoulder blades to shimmer like a star!

You've done your face, now you need to do your nails. A pop star has got to have nails to die for — so no bitten-down stumps for you. No way! Check out these top five tips for posh talons . . .

1. If your nails are too short (don't bite them!), you can press on false ones to disguise them. But if you don't want to wear false ones, just paint a clear polish on so you don't draw attention to them.

2. Use a good nail file to shape decent-sized nails — don't use a metal one. File in one direction only and do not use a sawing action — be gentle. Make sure your nails are clean before you paint them.

3. You are ready for polish. Colors are up to you, but you can add nail tattoos under polish and nail jewels on top of polish — the polish just needs to be wet so you can set the jewel on the nail.

4. If you want to go for colored polish, apply while your hand is resting on a magazine or something so it doesn't drip anywhere. Apply with one stroke on the center of

the nail and then one stroke on either side to finish. Any smudges can be cleaned up around the edge of the nail with a cotton swab dipped in remover.

5. If you want to make a real splash — paint half your nails one color, wait for it to dry, and then paint another color to contrast. You could paint stripes of one color on top of another. Paint a swirl on top of another color after it has dried. Paint each nail a different color, or with a fine paintbrush paint a letter on each nail to spell out words!

PSST! Gossip Britney bites her nails down to stumps! See — not everyone's perfect!

Luscious locks

Your hair is just soooo important if you are a pop star. Look how many times Madonna has changed hers, as well as Posh Spice going from mid-length to short to really long. You need to be able to keep changing — but how, without spending all your pocket money? Well . . . you could sweep your eyes over this collection of stunning styles that will make you stand out from the crowd and start setting new trends all over the world . . .

Top Ten hair accessories:
1. Butterfly clips in different sizes
2. Hair bands in different colors
3. Barrettes with diamonds and flowers

4. Spring beads or hair jewels (jewels on the end of metal coils)
5. Ponytail bands
6. Hair mascara
7. A string of leather or ribbon
8. Gloss, gel, and hair spray
9. Zigzag hair band (scrapes hair back from face)
10. Color gel and glitter or color spray

PSST! Gossip Did you know that Geri Halliwell's extensions come from several Filipino women and are dyed specially and woven into her own hair?

Braid attack

This looks really glam and different — good for on-stage or at a posh party. Obviously you have to have long hair. You will need to get some help with this one.

※ Make sure your hair is really clean and slightly damp.

※ Divide your hair into four or five sections, parting one section by your left ear and then working over your head to your right ear. Each section begins at your forehead and ends at the back of your neck.

※ Start to braid at the front of your head, working backwards. The first part needs to be like a French braid, attached to your head with the rest of it hanging free. Then move on to the next section and slowly move across your head to your right ear.

✳ Once all sections are braided, take the end of each braid and thread it through the top of another to make a loop. The loops should all cross over each other to make a pretty pattern.

✳ Use bobby pins to hold the ends in place, securing them close to the scalp.

Spiketastic

If you have short hair that has a bit of length all over, this one will work for you.

★ Comb some gel through your hair — it helps if your hair hasn't just been washed.

★ Take a small section of hair and tie it in a tiny bunch with a band, then move on to the next section.

★ When your whole head is covered in tiny bunches, that's when you attack it with the hair mascara!

★ Backcomb the hair a bit if it isn't standing up (it should cuz of the gel) and then brush the hair mascara on the spiky ends. You could also stick in hair jewels if you want to go completely over the top!

Froth head

✳ Gather up the front of your locks and secure them with a butterfly clip.

✳ Tie back the rest of your hair and backcomb. Spray both sections with a bit of hair spray to give it a bit of hold — it should be full of volume.

✳ For the finishing touch, pin random strands of the backcombed hair loosely around your crown for that messy, just got outta bed look.

Poodle bunch

How do us girls keep our hair off our faces during those dance routines? Why, the poodle bunch, of course . . .

✳ Take the front section of hair and pull it away from the face, towards the crown.

✳ Loosely twist the section a couple of times and secure it in a topknot using a ponytail band. Your hair should just fall over your shoulders.

PSST! Gossip Billie Piper's number one super-quick beauty tip is: "Let your hair dry naturally if you don't have time to dry it. Keep it behind your ears – that loose, wet look is in right now."

Do the twist

This looks better on shorter hair.

✦ Divide hair into sections, twist, and fasten at the top of your head using glittery clips, butterflies, or bobby pins.

✦ Backcomb the ends for a real spiky rock chick look and spray with hair spray.

✦ You could use a zigzag hair band and get the same result.

Quick fixes

✳ Short hair can be side-parted and pretty clips put in to keep the parting secure. Hair jewels can also keep hair parted — just slick some gel in first.

✳ When you braid hair, to make it look stunning, weave a string of leather or ribbon through the braid or braids afterwards.

✳ When you put your hair in a ponytail, slick it back first with some gloss and then thread the end of a thin ribbon through a bobby pin and start weaving it across your hair from ear to ear. Do the same with two other contrasting-colored ribbons and tie the ends under your ponytail. Fab.

✻ Part long hair in the middle and tie each section into a high ponytail. Knot each ponytail in on itself, so it's like a bun. Then pin the knots to the side of your head with bobby pins while the pulled-through ends are left spiky.

✻ For rock chick big hair, braid long hair while wet and leave to dry or dry with a dryer. Undo braids (you can do as many as you like) and separate with fingers. You can add hair jewels or clip a center parting, and frizz out the rest of the hair.

✻ If you're sick of karma beads, use them to tie your hair back instead of a band — they look original.

PSST! Gossip Beverly Cobella, top hairdresser to all the stars, says that combing mayonnaise through freshly washed hair, leaving it for ten minutes, and then washing will make it shimmer with health! It does work – honest.

 Right, that's all, folks. Of course now that you have the hair and the makeup of a superstar, you're going to need the clothes from the catwalk to match.

I think LaydeeB has got some hot looks lined up for you in chapter seven. Rock on, babes! And remember what Daphne and Celeste say: *"If you're having a bad hair day, a cute little hair accessory can hide a multitude of follicular sins!"*

7.
Spice up your life

If you're in a girl band, it's important to wear the right clothes to get you noticed. Having a certain look that's yours is the way forward on the track to stardom. If you all look the same it can be boring, but if there's something that links all the band members, then that really works.

> Now, sisters, you need the clothes and I am the LaydeeB to tell you how to get them at bargain-basement prices. Discover a whole new you lurking in the back of your wardrobe!

Jean genie

"Denim is very versatile for the dance routines we do, and it's comfortable." Sinead, B*Witched.

Denim is the biggest fashion statement you can

wear as a piece of clothing because you can dress it up with posh shoes and sparkly jewelry or go casual with running shoes and a sweatshirt.

Bleached beauties

So what clothes are the stars of the pop world sporting? Well, Destiny's Child, Britney, and Christina Aguilera are all wearing bleached denims. And you can do the very same — all you have to do is ask Mom or Dad if you can transform an old pair. You should get some help from a grown-up because bleach is nasty stuff and can burn you if it comes into contact with your skin.

✶ Wear really old clothes and rubber gloves so if you do splash it, it won't matter if it makes a mark. Do the deed in the bathtub — that way it won't make a mess.

✶ Make sure the jeans are clean and lie them flat in the dry tub. Pour bleach onto your jeans in a squirty pattern, not covering all of the blue — you want to still see some blue to contrast with the white. Turn them over and do the same to the back.

✶ You might want to just dye the bottoms of the jeans and create a gradual pattern up the leg, till there is no bleach at the top at all.

✱ Finally, when you have finished, you need to leave the jeans for a bit to let the bleach work. When the pattern has developed, that's when you wash them in the hot cycle in the washing machine. Now you have a pair of jeans that no one else will — true designer jeans!

PSST! Gossip Even pop stars have fashion disasters: "Once I wore this black bodysuit and skirt. It was, like, really ugly. And the skirt was so tight it split when I bent over!" Beyoncé, Destiny's Child.

Super flares

You ain't no one unless you got a pair of flared jeans — no girl band should be without a pair. I own at least five pairs. I know Fazza and Kym have a million pairs each. Feast your eyes here . . .

❖ Take an old pair of jeans that your mom won't mind you cutting up. Grab a pair of scissors and get an adult to help cut up the seam on the outside of each leg. Be careful not to snip the material, but just the stitching that holds the seams together.

❖ Once you have snipped about six to eight inches — stop! Sew over the ends of the thread where you have cut so the jeans don't unravel even more.

Now you have jeans with a split up the side of each leg. You can leave them like this — they look cool — or go on to the next stage.

❖ Choose some cool-looking material — you can buy remnants in fabric stores, or maybe your mom has some lying around. Funky patterns, flowers, sequins, leather — anything that isn't denim!

❖ Stretch out the two seams you have just cut to decide how big you want the flares to be. Then measure the gap between the two seams and cut the other material to fit just over the area that will be the extra flare. You will need to hem the bottom of the material so it doesn't fray. Now sew the material between the two seams, sewing along each seam to disguise the stitches.

❖ Iron them and now you have a pair of customized mega-flares ready to do some serious dancing in.

Easy stuff . . .

✳ Got a pair of jeans or pants that look too plain? Draw a pattern on them in marker, around the pockets, bottoms, anywhere. Buy some pretty beads and sequins from a craft store and get sewing, following the pattern you made. Beware! Only do small patterns, one at a time, because it can get very tedious sewing all those beads on!

❋ Jazz up a pair of old jeans with sequin trim. Just sew it on around pockets, down the sides of the jeans, or along the bottoms. Easier than individual beads.

❋ Fray jeans by cutting along the bottom and putting them through the wash a few times.

PSST! Gossip Christina Aguilera's top fashion tip: "When I'm not on TV or in front of a camera, then I always wear a bandanna. It helps hide the fact I haven't done my hair!"

Tight T's

Tight T-shirts really are the secret to looking cool if you ask me. They look fab with baggy pants, a pencil skirt, jeans — just about everything. So do little vest tops. If you have some that you never wear anymore — they've got a stain or you're just sick of the sight — well, help is at hand . . .

❋ Dye old T's different colors for each of you in the band. Get an adult to help.

GIRL BAND

✳ Draw the name of the band, or your own names, on each T, then sew sequin trim around the letters and spell out your name sparkly style. You now look like the newest girl band to hijack the charts!

✳ Buy a cheap feather boa and cut it up and sew it around the necks, bottoms, or sleeves of old T's. You could do all three if you want to look like a real rock chick!

✳ Attack dark T's with bleach like you did with the jeans — make sure they're cotton, though.

✳ Sew a shape on the front of your T in the same material as the flares in your jeans to make a whole outfit. Add sequins and beads.

✳ Wind sequin trim around the straps of old undershirts.

✳ Design a band logo on paper or on the computer, take it to a copy shop with your T-shirts, and get it printed on the front of the shirts.

✳ Sew a strip of Velcro onto a plain T and then cut out letters from some colored felt. Make up your own slogans and phrases to go across the front.

✳ Get a grown-up to slash zigzag patterns with a sharp knife (eek!) in the front of old T's and either leave for the disheveled look or sew funky material behind the slashes. Rock on . . .

PSST! Gossip Spotted at the MTV Europe awards — Madonna wearing a Kylie Minogue T-shirt held together with safety pins. Spotted at her first concert in years in the US — Madonna wearing a Britney Spears T-shirt. Spotted out shopping — Britney in a Madonna T-shirt. A new craze has been born!

You girls might wanna wear skirts, and I haven't really mentioned them cuz if you are a true girl band and you wanna strut your funky stuff, then dancing in a skirt is quite hard. You can adapt any ideas for skirts here, but remember — you won't be able to jump in the air gracefully without showing your undies!

Accessory heaven

Don't get onstage without at least one of these:

* A scarf to keep hair out of the way
* Karma beads to match your mood
* Beaded or feather choker
* Body jewels — look good when stuck on a midriff around the bellybutton
* Silver rings, toe rings, thumb rings, fake tummy piercings
* Studded leather wrist cuffs
* Skinny studded belt or glitter belt

* Ankle bracelet, ear cuffs
* Fake diamond cross
* Chunky shoes, sandals, or high boots
* Sunglasses
* Fake tattoos. Buy body art kits or henna tattoo kits so you can draw your own designs. Always follow the instructions. You could try some of these designs to paint on tummies and arms — even your feet!

PSST! Gossip Spicy Mel C might be regretting her tattoos: "When I first started getting tattoos I didn't even think. Now I'm starting to panic how I'll look in twenty years." Go fake every time, we say!

 Now you have everything — the makeup, the hair, the clothes — just put it all together and what have you got? Take a look and see . . .

Rock chick

Wears: Bleached flared jeans and cowboy boots or stiletto shoes, animal-print undershirt, and either leather funnel-neck jacket or bleached denim jacket.

Accessories: Fake tattoos, fake diamond cross necklace, thumb ring, wrist cuffs, studded belt.

Hair: Spiky and short or a bright color with ear cuffs showing.

Makeup: Glossy pink lips, bit of glitter on chest, and lots of dark eye makeup with black-lined eyes and mascara.

Nails: Red with fake diamonds stuck on them!

Urban rap chick

Wears: Baggy hipster pants with pockets, chunky shoes, tight designer T-shirt, hooded sweatshirt, and body warmer.

Accessories: Wraparound sunglasses, thumb ring, tattoos, funky watch, silver ring, ear cuff.

Hair: Chin-length style twisted into clips and butterflies, or zigzag hair band scraping it back from her face and spiky at the back.

Makeup: Natural look with lip gloss and a bit of brown eye shadow and mascara.

Nails: Tattoos with clear polish.

Slick chick

Wears: Tight hip-hugger-style flared trousers or pencil skirt, high boots or strappy sandals, tight handkerchief top showing off midriff.

Accessories: Fake diamond cross, glitter belt, silver bangle, toe ring, ankle bracelet.

Hair: Either scraped back with spiky bits at the back, short and slicked back, or long and luscious with maybe a few highlights.

Makeup: Silver or gold eyes with another subtle color to highlight, mascara, glossy pink lips, bronzed cheeks and shoulders, and maybe glitter too.

Nails: Natural with maybe a pink tinge or bindis on the thumbs.

Hippy chick

Wears: Frayed flared beaded jeans, gypsy-style top, chunky shoes or sandals, beaded cardigan.

Accessories: Feather choker, ear cuff, karma beads, bindi, toe ring, ankle bracelet, tattoos.

Hair: Probably long, either in braids or loose with jewels in it and, of course, a head scarf! If short, hair jewels and butterfly clips.

Makeup: Pink or browny-red lips, pink cheeks, eye jewels, and mascara.

Nails: Purple and silver nails with patterns on them.

SPICE UP YOUR LIFE

PSST! Gossip Did you know that Britney has an obsession about buying sunglasses? She always buys a pair when she goes out.

You've checked out your basic looks. You don't have to stick to any style; these are just guides to help you get a look together. If you want more help, just check out magazines and watch TV — there's loads of info on fashion and style and gossip. Try these web sites for copying the looks of the stars: www.swizzle.co.uk or www.mykindaplace.com. Have you spotted me on there . . . ?

PSST! Gossip Take a page out of All Saints Shaznay's book: "Don't wear clothes just because they're trendy. If you're not into what you you're wearing it'll stand out a mile."

8.
S Club party

Now's the time for you to show off what you've been up to. Time for your public to see how amazingly talented you are and to witness your Out of This World dance routines. It's show time!!!!!!

Party with the stars

Yeah, laydees, time for your showcase. Hmm . . . what's a showcase? A showcase is what all new bands have after a record company has just signed them. It's like a mini concert, but not so scary cuz there are not so many people there — mostly music journalists from newspapers and magazines. Sometimes the showcase is so small they hold it in the studio where they recorded the album, so you could call it a party. All bands have had showcases — the Spice Girls, B*Witched, Westlife, Backstreet Boys.

Edele from B*Witched says of her first showcase: "It was the most nerve-wracking thing I've ever had to do, but our families were there, so it made it easier." But you will be having fun with all your friends; there'll be no nasty music executives to scare you off!

Lots of stars have lucky charms or rituals before they go onstage. Britney says a prayer and her . . . er . . . good friend Justin from 'N Sync puts peppermint oil under his nose to help him breathe easier! What would you do? Rub your lucky rabbit's foot?

So how can you have a showcase? Easy! All you need to do is majorly grovel to Mom or Dad for use of the biggest room in the house — sometimes, the garage is better because it doesn't matter if you make a mess. As if . . .

PSST! Gossip You know you've made it big when your hometown wants to open a museum dedicated to you. Yes, Britney again! Residents in her hometown, Kentwood, Louisiana, are doing just that to celebrate her life.

Get bizzy with it

Time to organize yourselves like an army of ants. Get those invites out; make sure they are glitzy with as much glitter as possible. Add stick-on jewels and bindis so they look like individual works of art. You want people to get excited, don't you?

Next is the room. You need it to look like the sort of place a band would have a showcase. A bit of glamor would be wicked, so you need to create an atmosphere. If it's in the garage or the living room, our top tip is to buy drop cloths from a hardware store. You are going to make the backdrop to your stage.

✴ Tuck the drop cloths over the top of the curtains at one end of the room so they cover them completely. If you're in the garage, see if you can hang them off the garage door.

✴ Have lots of paper handy — now you are going to cut out stars and the name of your group and any other words in big letters. Spray the stars and words gold or silver and add glitter if you want (you know it makes sense!). Stick them on the sheets with double-sided tape.

✴ On the floor in front of the backdrop, mark out a rectangle with masking tape — that is your stage. Make sure you have enough room to do your routine. You don't want to fall off the stage now, do you? To add that special touch, borrow as many flashlights as you can and stand them around the edge of your stage area. Now how cool does that look when they're all switched on?

✳ Hang stars and moons over the stage and/or whatever else you can think of. Use leftover stars and shapes that have been sprayed silver or gold on both sides and thread them onto pieces of see-through fishing line — you can buy it in hardware stores — by making a hole in the top of each shape with a needle. Now attach them to the ceiling with tape.

PSST! Gossip Stars sometimes have trouble onstage: Yonah from girl band Cleopatra once wasn't looking where she was going on the stage and slipped down the stairs on her rear end in front of everyone! Embarrassing . . .

Now all you need are flashing lights for your show-case! You can rent them from disco and sound equip-ment stores, or a grown-up could buy them and keep them for other parties (they are not too expensive and you could ask for them as a birthday present). However, the cheap option would be to bribe little brothers and sisters to hold torches at the back and swirl them over the ceiling!

Rehearsing is vital. You need to know the limita-tions of the stage you have created on the floor and might have to adjust old routines to fit the space. You will also have made a tape from CDs of the songs you are to perform. Between each song, leave a couple of seconds' gap so you can catch your breath and get into the starting position for the next number. Make sure you have someone starting and stopping the tape for you so you are all onstage at the beginning; you don't want to be bothered with worrying about the music. Also — it won't look as professional. Remember to relax and do a few vocal warmups before you perform. Try the humming exercises from chapter four.

PSST! Gossip You don't want to be like Nicole from All Saints who forgot to go onstage cuz she was gossiping too much and missed her cue. She had no shoes on, either!

That's it! You've sent out the invites but you can't just have a party about you, can you? You aren't Destiny's Child just yet, so you won't be able to keep your audience entertained for hours on end, will you? Well, no, BUT they could entertain themselves. Check these out . . .

Sing it back

You may be the only ones with a rehearsed routine, but everyone has a bit of pop star in them, don't they? You can bet all your friends do and they might be a tad jealous watching you strut your funky booty onstage, so why not let them join in? Yes — beg, plead, do the dishes for a week, even walk the dog in the rain, just so you can rent a karaoke machine! You know you wanna. What fun — watching your friends screech their way through "Baby One More Time" and outdoing drowning cats with tuneful renditions of "Bring It All Back." If you can't rent a karaoke machine, buy one of the CDs, like the one you've used for your backing track, photocopy all the word sheets, and buy a microphone that you plug into your stereo. Microphones are very cheap; just make sure your stereo has an output for one.

PSST! Gossip Jo from S Club 7's hobby is singing karaoke!

To make it even more entertaining, have surplus accessories that the other "acts" can dress up in: feather boas, tiaras, hats, wigs, and a ton of body glitter.

Disco divas

Oh, yes — that competition that always induces fights, squabbles, and broken friendships! But it's worth it just to get on down and boogie. Have a dancing competition with prizes. The judge has to be someone not involved at ALL, like an older brother/sister, parent, etc. Everyone starts dancing in the style of someone like Britney or B*Witched and one by one, the judge will eliminate everyone, until there are just two people left for a Give It All You Got finale. Obviously, there are no rules, just that the best dancer wins. If you want to be in with a chance, check out the dance moves in chapter five.

PSST! Gossip Jessica Simpson's most embarrassing moment: "I auditioned for *The Mickey Mouse Club* and it was a disaster. I forgot every song – I might as well have been picking my nose!"

You'll all want to sit down after you've danced your legs off, so why not have a quiz to test all your A–Z of pop knowledge. Try some of these questions, but it's really easy to make up your own out of magazines and off band web sites on the Internet. You'll need loads more questions anyway if you want your quiz to last more than five seconds!

Pop quiz

Split up into teams named after your fave girl pop band or performer and have a Quiz Master read out the questions. If someone knows the answer to a question, they have to shout out the name of their team first.

1. Which other teen queen started off as a Mousketeer on The Mickey Mouse Club with Britney Spears?
a) Mariah Carey
b) Christina Aguilera
c) Jessica Simpson

2. Give the FULL names of all five original members of the Spice Girls.

3. What is the name of Posh Spice's baby?
a) Brandon
b) Brooklyn
c) Birmingham

4. What is the name of S Club 7's TV show?
a) LA 7
b) NY 7
c) UK 7

5. Where did S Club 7's show used to be filmed?
a) Madrid
b) Miami
c) Montreal

S CLUB PARTY

6. Which country does Samantha Mumba come from?
a) America
b) England
c) Ireland

7. Name Christina Aguilera's first number one hit.
a) "Lucky"
b) "Genie in a Bottle"
c) "What a Girl Wants"

8. Who are the twins in B*Witched?
a) Keavy and Edele
b) Sinead and Lindsay
c) Keavy and Lindsay

9. Which prince was supposed to have a crush on Britney?
a) Harry
b) William
c) Charles

10. Which famous pop diva did Westlife duet with?
a) Whitney Houston
b) Madonna
c) Mariah Carey

GIRL BAND

11. Who is the youngest S Clubber?
a) Jonathan
b) Bradley
c) Hannah

12. Which Spice Girl had a chart-topper with rocker Bryan Adams?
a) Posh
b) Mel B
c) Mel C

13. Who isn't a mother in All Saints?
a) Shaznay
b) Nicole and Natalie
c) Mel

14. Name the Spice Girls' third album
a) Always
b) Forever
c) Goodbye

15. Which film did Destiny's Child sing the theme song to?
a) Charlie's Angels
b) The Grinch
c) Stuart Little

Investigate some of these sites for star trivia:
S Club 7, **www.sclub.com**

S CLUB PARTY

Britney, **www.britneyspears.com**

Spice Girls, **www.c3.vmg.co.uk/spicegirls**

Backstreet Boys, **www.backstreetboys.com**

Westlife, **www.westlife.co.uk**

B*Witched, **www.b-witched.com**

Steps, **www.stepsofficial.com**

Madonna, **www.madonnafanclub.com**

Destiny's Child, **www.destinyschild.com**

For quiz questions and facts on up-to-the-minute bands, check these sites:

www.canwidecirculation.com/AllPop/trivia facts.html, www.dotmusic.com

I could write out a million questions for you, but that's not the point! You have to think of them yourselves and create your own personal quiz. Don't groan — it's fun! Use these questions as a guide to the sort of questions you are gonna ask. See the answers below.

Get any right?

1. b 2. Geri Halliwell, Melanie Chisholm, Victoria Beckham, Emma Bunton, Melanie Brown 3. b 4. a 5. b 6. c. 7. b. 8. a 9. b 10. c 11. a 12. c 13. a 14. b 15. c

There's loads of other stuff you can do at your show-case after you have done your thang. Get handy with that magic wand on your friends . . .

Celebrity makeovers

Transform your friends into the pop stars of their choice. Pile up those magazines and, using the make-up tips from this book, copy their looks. Britney is all dark eyes and lots of eyeliner, with pink lips and sparkly eye shadow. She says her fave eye shadow is brown, with a dark brown on the lid and a lighter one brushed on her brow bone. Posh goes for maximum makeup coverage with glossy lips and eyes as her trademark and VERY tight clothes. B*Witched always look casual, with glitter for glamour, but don't forget their uniform of denim. Now, who wants to be Madonna . . . ?

Who am I?

After you are all made up, you can play the celebrity name-guessing game. Sit in a circle and each of you write down the name of a pop star on a Post-it Note and stick it on the head of the person next to you, making sure they don't see who it is. Each person has to ask a question to the group about the person she is (Am I a girl? Am I in a group?). If they guess correctly, they get to ask another question. If not, the next player has a turn. The winner is the first person to guess what name is on her Post-it Note.

PSST! Gossip Did you know that many celebrities endorse all sorts of products? Britney has a hair accessory, fanny pack, and doll; Christina has her own self-adorned lunch box; and the Spice Girls have their own dolls and Cadbury chocolates with their signatures on the wrappers!

Have a posh party! All showcases have nibbles (in pop star circles they are called canapés, dahling) on trays handed out by waiters — you wanna look like true stars, don'tcha? Get a grown-up to help you out with the food side of things. Give these canapé ideas a whirl: mini sausage rolls, tiny cucumber sandwiches with the crusts cut off, cheese swirls (see recipe below), tortilla chips with salsa and sour cream dips, mini spring rolls (you can buy them ready-made), pizzas cut up into neat squares. Basically, the word here is MINI. As long as it's small and you can fit it in your mouth in one bite, it can be a canapé! You might have to bribe younger brothers and sisters to hand out food like those waiters . . .

Cheese swirls

This is a yummy party food and soooo quick to make. You will need help with this from a grown-up.

Roll out a pack of store-bought puff pastry till it's about a quarter of an inch thick. Grate enough sharp cheese to cover the whole area of pastry and then roll it up into a sausage. Now slice off discs of this pastry roll and place them on a greased baking sheet. Bake in a medium-hot oven (350°F) till they are golden brown. You can make pizza swirls by spreading tomato paste on the pastry before you add the cheese.

"Cocktails"

If they're having a showcase, most bands drink champagne, but you're too young. BUT, you can have fruit "cocktails" instead. For strawberry cocktails, whiz some strawberries in a blender and add to orange juice with loads of ice. For a banana surprise, mash a banana with blended strawberry and mix with milk and vanilla ice cream. There are loads of combos you can make — orange and banana; coconut milk, orange juice, and strawberry; banana, cranberry, and orange juice; Coke and orange juice (!). Just experiment before you try them out on any of your friends — you don't want to poison them.

PSST! Gossip Britney loves making smoothies. Get a grown-up to whiz vanilla ice cream and soft fruit like strawberries or bananas in a blender and experience a Britney

Smoothie! Hannah from S Club 7 has a fave smoothie recipe: five strawberries, a banana, orange juice, and a scoop of ice cream all blended together for a cool S Club "cocktail."

You've got loads of action planned for your showcase party — enough to keep everyone amused. The main thing to remember is to give it all you've got while performing and have a scream. You are entertaining your audience and yourselves!

9.
A star is born

We all started somewhere and we've just given you your start on the road to fame and fortune . . . well, an idea for a pretty cool party, anyway. How do you think your favorite pop stars burst onto the music scene? Was it overnight, or was it years of hard work and sweat, singing in gross clubs and bars? Well, why don'tcha look and see . . .

All things nice

Why don't we begin with the one and only Spice Girls? They are (fingers crossed) still together, but rumors fly every day that our fave girl band is about to call it quits. Maybe they will, maybe they won't, but here's how it all started. . . .

Posh, Ginger, Baby, Scary, and Sporty all met as far back as 1993 at various unsuccessful auditions for singing and dancing jobs, and they ended up sharing a house in Maidenhead, Berkshire, in the UK. When manager Simon Fuller took them on in 1995, they had already started writing songs and making demo tapes. A record contract with Virgin swiftly followed and by June 1996 their first single, "Wannabe," was on its way to number one in the UK. By February 1997 they had made it to number one in the US, making history as the first UK act to make the top of the American mag *Billboard* with their debut album.

Toward the end of '97 they fired Simon Fuller, and everyone thought they would sink without a trace. Oh, ye of little faith — it takes more than that to break the Spices! To prove their popularity, their movie, *Spice World,* was released on December 26, 1997, and was a monster hit all around the world. The number one singles kept coming as did the Spice Dolls, chocolates, jewelry, T-shirts, books . . . you name it, there was a Spice Girl with it! But suddenly something awful happened just before their world tour: Geri left the band! How were they going to cope without their Girl Power leader? Well, just fine, it seemed. Life went on, and they continued their world domination with a sellout tour, coming back to Britain to rest, get married (Posh and Scary!), have babies (Posh and Scary), and do solo projects (Sporty and Scary). It looked like they might split, but no — the new millennium saw a more grown-up Spice Girls with the release of their third album, *Forever.* This started a famous battle with boy band Westlife in the UK charts, ending up with both bands declaring chart and personal warfare on each other. Now, that's not very ladylike, girls! The Spice Girls are still going strong at the moment, but for how long with all these up-and-coming teen stars ready and waiting to steal their crown?

Take a page out of Destiny's Child's book and work really hard to get to the top. The younger you start (they were only nine and ten!), the easier it will get later on with all that experience behind you. Did you do the quiz in chapter three? Could you handle school and singing and dancing every day till you make it big? Check this out . . .

Independent women

Destiny's Child is the BIGGEST girl band in the world at the moment. Go girls! They had a number one single, "Independent Women Part One," in December 2000. However, the trio, consisting of Beyoncé Knowles, Michelle Williams, and Kelly Rowland, didn't always have the same lineup as they do now. The Destiny's Child story began in 1990 in Houston, when friends Beyoncé and LaTavia Robertson hooked up with Beyoncé's cousin Kelly Rowland. They spent afternoons studying videos of the Jackson Five and the Supremes to mimic their dance routines. Two years later, LaToya Luckett joined the group and, with the final member in place, the girls found they had a special chemistry.

Coming up with a cool name was proving tricky, but fate intervened. One day Beyoncé's mother picked up the Bible and a picture fell out with the word "Destiny" in the title. They adapted this to Destiny's Children and then shortened it to Destiny's Child.

Armed with their fab new name and Beyoncé's dad acting as their manager, the group kick-started their career with a performance on *Star Search*. The girls were pitched against acts nearly three times their age, and while they didn't win, it certainly got the ball rolling. LaTavia recalls the show: *"We were kind of nervous about it. They made us do a rap song, although we wanted to sing."* Gradually, low-profile appearances in and around Houston led to Destiny's Child supporting bigger and bigger acts when they came to town. By 1996, the group had signed with a record company, and all those years of hard work finally paid off when their first single, "Killing Time," from their debut album appeared on the sound track of the Will Smith film *Men in Black*. Their second album in 1999 was a massive seller and from there on, they climbed to dizzy heights with many hits, including "Say My Name," "Bills, Bills, Bills," and "Jumpin', Jumpin'." Now megastars, award winners, and famous all over the world (and still with an average age of eighteen!), the group faced a crisis point. In March 2000, LaTavia and LaToya left the group but were immediately replaced by nineteen-year-old Michelle Williams and eighteen-year-old Farrah Franklin! That's the pop music merry-go-round for you! Well, after five months with Destiny's Child, Farrah also quit! And this is where we end up, ten years later (!), with the talented trio we know and love — our kung-fu-kicking funky angels who are storming the charts and carrying on in the Girl Power tradition. We salute you, Destiny's Child!

 See — you can do it too. Entering competitions is the way to go if you are serious about wanting to be famous. Just make sure you can sing! Singing into the bathroom mirror is a good start, just like Britney used to when she was five years old . . .

Mickey Mouse paves the way . . .

So how did the Britney Spears phenomenon kick off all those years ago? *"When I was a little girl, I was always performing. I remember buying* Thriller *[Michael Jackson's album] and I used to dance around the room all the time."* From as far back as she could remember, Britney had always wanted to sing and dance and attended dance and gymnastic classes. At age nine, Britney learned that the Disney Channel was holding auditions for *The Mickey Mouse Club*. Britney shone like a star when she met the producers, but she was deemed too young to be a Mouseketeer and was pointed in the direction of an agent instead. Soon after the audition, Britney, her mom, and her little sister, Jamie Lynn, left Kentwood, Louisiana, to move to the Hell's Kitchen neighborhood of New York to help nurture Britney's artistic talents. While there, every summer she attended the Off-Broadway Dance Center and the Professional Performing Arts School and was soon landing parts in TV commercials and Off-Broadway shows. Like Destiny's Child, she also entered *Star Search* — and won!

At eleven, Britney was now old enough to reapply for *The New Mickey Mouse Club* and she landed the coveted spot of a Mouseketeer. As well as Britney, there were other Mouseketeers with bright futures: Christina Aguilera, and JC Chasez and Justin Timberlake, both from 'N Sync. It was during her time on *The New Mickey Mouse Club* that Britney realized she wanted to pursue a career in music. After two years Britney handed back her Mouse ears and returned to Kentwood for a normal year in high school, but was soon wishing she was off traveling the world, performing for audiences. Britney decided to audition for girl group Innosense in a bid to achieve her dream as a pop star. As usual, she stood out for being so brilliant (go, Britney!), but the manager of the group wouldn't take her — he thought she was too talented! For real! He sent Britney's demo tape to Jive records, where they immediately saw her potential and offered her a record deal.

After recording her album in Sweden, Britney came home and was sent on a national tour of shopping malls, like Debbie Gibson and Tiffany had done in the eighties. But instead of becoming a one-hit wonder, Britney was mobbed everywhere she went, and when she brought out her debut single in 1998, *Baby One More Time*, there was Britney mania! She had a hit all over the world and her album was a mega success internationally. It was the start of the Britney roller coaster. Her second album, *Oops! . . . I*

Did It Again! was released in 2000 and Britney commenced a world tour for the first time. All this and only nineteen years old! This just proves that teens continue to rule the school!

PSST! Gossip

So, you now have an idea of how much hard work being a pop star involves. Do you still want to do it? All stars have similar stories of grueling tours, initial poverty, no privacy, and not much sleep. Madonna had only $37 in her pocket when she arrived in New York to make it in the record industry. She was reduced to eating leftover fast food from garbage cans when she ran out of money! Farrah Franklin was rumored to have left Destiny's Child cuz she couldn't cope with their schedule. Other pop stars had very unglamorous jobs before they made the big time: Keavy Lynch from B*Witched worked as a car mechanic before she joined the group, and Geri Halliwell was a game show hostess on TV. But if you wanted fame badly enough, you'd be willing to put up with all these things and do anything, wouldn't you . . . ?

That's all our advice on everything you need to know about being in a girl band. Remember to keep practicing those routines and laugh. We all had to start somewhere and now you know how some of the biggest stars in the galaxy made their way to superstardom. We want to hear good things about you!

10. Knowing me, knowing you

You've been given loads of advice and heard about everyone else out there playing the fame game, dancing the dance, talking the talk, and wearing the latest clothes. But what about you? We don't know anything about you! We wanna know!

Girl Band Press Release

Fill in this section of the book and keep it as a souvenir of your time in a girl band.

Your band name

_____

Members of the band

_____

_____

_____

_____

_____

Your band picture

Your favorite song you perform

_____

Your most embarrassing moments in the band

_____

_____

KNOWING ME, KNOWING YOU

_____

_____

_____

_____

Where was your first performance?

_____

Have you had any pop star problems yet?

_____

_____

_____

_____

_____

List your favorite outfits

_____

_____

_____

_____

_____

GIRL BAND

If you could film a pop video anywhere in the world, where would you go?

_____

_____

What would you have in your dressing room at a concert (e.g. pizzas, soda machine, personal assistant, etc!)?

_____

_____

_____

_____

_____

_____

Who are your top five favorite bands or pop stars?

_____

_____

_____

_____

_____

Which pop stars should be banished to outer space?

_____

_____

_____

KNOWING ME, KNOWING YOU

If you could record a single with anyone, who would it be?

_____

_____

Name the best-dressed pop star ever.

_____

Backstreet Boys or 'N Sync?

_____

Neither! Girls rule!

Name your top ten favorite songs of all time.

_____

_____

_____

_____

_____

_____

_____

_____

Name your top five least favorites!

Last piece of advice before the end of the book — practice your autographs! It took me ages to perfect mine. You never know when someone will ask you to sign, or what they will want you to sign. I heard Edele from B*Witched had to sign a diaper for a fan! Hope it hadn't been used.

Good luck and have fun with the book. Try not to fall over onstage and all will be cool! We know you are going to be GREAT! Byeeeeee!